CHICKEN, CHICKEN, DUCK!

BY **Nadia Krilanovich**

TRICYCLE PRESS
Berkeley

Chicken

Chicken

Duck

Goat

Sheep

Llama

maa maa

baa baa

snuffle

cluck . . .

QUACK!

Chicken

Chicken

Duck

Horse

Pig

Cow

neigh neigh

grunt grunt

QUACK!

Chicken

Chicken

Duck

Mouse

Cat

Dog

QUACK!

Look at all

the animals

standing in a stack!

QUACK!

For Mom, Dad, J, G, H, and M—you lucky ducks!

With special thanks to Kim—editor, collaborator, and advocate.

All rights reserved. Published in the United States by Tricycle Press, an imprint of Random House Children's Books, a division of Random House, Inc., New York. www.randomhouse.com/kids

Tricycle Press and the Tricycle Press colophon are registered trademarks of Random House, Inc.

Library of Congress Cataloging-in-Publication Data

Krilanovich, Nadia.
  Chicken, chicken, duck! / by Nadia Krilanovich. — 1st ed.
     p. cm.
  Summary: Easy-to-read, rhythmic text about a group of farm animals, led by a tenacious duck, who play a noisy game together.
  [1. Games—Fiction. 2. Ducks—Fiction. 3. Domestic animals—Fiction. 4. Animal sounds—Fiction.] I. Title.
  PZ7.K8964Chi 2011
  [E—dc22

                               2010010773

ISBN 978-1-58246-385-8 (hardcover)
ISBN 978-1-58246-389-6 (Gibraltar lib. bdg.)

Printed in Malaysia

Design by Colleen Cain
The type of this book is set in Imprimerie.
The illustrations were rendered in acrylics on paper.

1 2 3 4 5 6 – 16 15 14 13 12 11

First Edition